O9-AIG-189

A NOTE ABOUT THE STORY

My Irish grandfather, Thomas Lawrence Downey, was a great storyteller. I loved his rendition of The Animal Fair and his explanation of why he was bald (*that* will remain a personal secret). I never tired of sitting on his knee—and later, when I was a bit too big, sitting on the floor at his feet with one of my baby sisters on his knee—listening to his wonderful tall tales.

Among the stories I loved the best were the ones about the Irish —and the Downey family in particular. In those tales, I'm afraid, "dramatic flair" and artistic liberties took over for fact. But as any good storyteller knows, to embellish is to make the tale interesting, especially to a young Tomie.

When I read the short tale that inspired *Jamie O'Rourke and the Big Potato*, I swear I could hear my grandfather Tom Downey whispering in my ear, "Jamie O'Rourke was the laziest man...." Now I hope that the next generation, sitting on someone's knees or at someone's feet, will hear the words just as I did.

— Tomie dePaola, Creative Director
WHITEBIRD BOOKS

to Sharyn

Jamie O'Rourke and the Big Potato

An Irish folktale retold and illustrated by

TOMIE dePAOLA

Tomie '93

A WHITEBIRD BOOK
G. P. Putnam's Sons
New York

For my Irish buddy, John Sullivan.

Copyright © 1992 by Tomie dePaola
All rights reserved. This book, or parts thereof, may not be reproduced
in any form without permission in writing from the publisher.
G. P. Putnam's Sons, a division of The Putnam & Grosset Book Group,
200 Madison Avenue, New York, NY 10016.
Published simultaneously in Canada.
Printed in Hong Kong by South China Printing Co. (1988) Ltd.
Book design by Gunta Alexander
Library of Congress Cataloging-in-Publication Data
dePaola, Tomie. Jamie O'Rourke and the big potato : an Irish folktale /
retold and illustrated by Tomie dePaola. p. cm. "A Whitebird Book."
Summary: The laziest man in all of Ireland catches a leprechaun,
who offers a potato seed instead of a pot of gold for his freedom.
[1. Folklore – Ireland.] I. Title. PZ8.1.D43Jam 1991 398.2 – dc20 [E] 91-10626 CIP AC
ISBN 0-399-22257-X
1 3 5 7 9 10 8 6 4 2
First Impression

Jamie O'Rourke was the laziest man in all of Ireland.
He would do anything to avoid working, especially if it had
to do with growing potatoes.

"Jamie O'Rourke," his wife, Eileen, would say. "We'll have nothing to eat this winter if you don't go out and dig up the praties."

"Oh, the saints preserve us," Jamie would whine. "Me back's as sore as can be. Sure as I'm tellin' you, wife, you'll have to dig them up yourself. I'll break in two if I so much as get up out of this bed."

So Eileen, who had done all the planting and watering and weeding anyhow, would go out to the tiny garden and dig up the smallest potatoes in Ireland, all because Jamie was too lazy to dig a larger garden and had no money to buy good potato seed.

Then poor Eileen wrenched her back and was laid up in bed.
"St. Bridget and the Virgin Mary herself must have smiled
on Eileen O'Rourke," the village women said. "Why, it's the
first rest she's had since she married Jamie O'Rourke."

With Eileen in bed, Jamie began to worry. No Eileen to dig meant no praties all winter, and no praties meant no food.

"Oh, poor me," wailed Jamie. "I'll starve to death. I'd best go to church and confess to Father O'Malley. There's no telling how soon old Death will be knockin' on me door."

So, even though it was midnight, Jamie set out for the church. He was about halfway down the hill when he heard singing and a tap, tap, tapping sound.

"Sure and I wouldn't be knowin'," Jamie whispered, "but I swear it's a leprechaun." And sure enough, sitting in a circle of ferns in the moonlight was a leprechaun singing and hammering tiny nails into the heels of the fairy boots he was making. Jamie knew just what to do.

He crept up and grabbed the little man by his coattails
and held firm.

"Let me go! Let me go!" the leprechaun shouted.

"Not on your life," Jamie said. "Not until you show me
where you keep your pot of gold."

Now, everyone in Ireland knows that leprechauns make
boots and dancing shoes for the fairies, who pay for them with
gold. And everyone knows that if you catch a leprechaun, he'll
pay for his freedom with his pot of gold. But this leprechaun
was cleverer than most.

"Oh, please, Mr. Mortal Man," he pleaded. "I'm just startin'
out makin' fairy shoes and I only have one or two pieces of
gold in my pot. Won't you take a wish instead?"

"Why, what would I wish for?" Jamie asked. "Me who's about to die of starvation because my wife is sick in bed and can't dig the praties for the winter. And they're such puny praties anyhow."

"Well," said the leprechaun, reaching into his pocket, "you could wish for the biggest pratie in the world. It would last all winter and you wouldn't have to do anything more than plant this seed, water it, and wait."

That sounded wonderful to Jamie. "Done!" he shouted, and as the leprechaun dropped the seed into Jamie's hand, Jamie let go of his coattails and off that leprechaun scampered.

When Eileen heard what he had done, she was furious. "Jamie O'Rourke, you're not only the laziest man in Ireland, but a fool as well. Givin' up a pot of gold for a pratie seed!"

"Well, I'm going to plant this seed and water it and you'll see," Jamie said, and out he went.

And, faith, Eileen did see. In no time at all the biggest, finest potato plant had sprouted out of the ground followed by the potato itself. It was so big it pushed up not only all the dirt in the garden, but the garden shed and the corner of the cottage as well.

"Well, surely now it's ready to dig," Jamie said proudly.

He hoed all around it, but he couldn't dig that pratie out of the ground. He got a beam and a big rock and tried to pry it out. He pushed and he pushed, but it wouldn't budge.

As he was pondering what to do, his neighbor passed by on his way to the village. He couldn't believe his eyes. He couldn't wait to tell everyone in the village what he had seen. And before you knew it, the hill up to Jamie's was filled with villagers coming to see the big potato.

"Where did it come from?" they asked.

Jamie told them about the lucky night he had caught the leprechaun and how smart he had been. "Why, anyone could have gotten a pot of gold," he bragged. "But the biggest pratie in the world, well that took some doin'!"

"However did you outsmart a leprechaun?" they all asked at once. Jamie hesitated and scratched his head. "We'll help you dig up your pratie, Jamie, if you'll tell us how you did it!" And they grabbed shovels and hoes and started to dig.

They dug and they dug, and they pushed and they shoved until the potato flew up out of its hole. It rolled down the hill, faster and faster until it reached the bottom where it bounced up high and came to a stop, wedged between the stone walls on either side of the road.

What to do now?

"That pratie is so big that no one, no cart, nothin' can get by it," the constable complained to Father O'Malley. "How's a body to get in or out of the village?"

"What shall we do?" the villagers wailed.

Then they all looked at Jamie and said, "It's your pratie.
You'll have to move it out of our way."

"Well," Eileen spoke up, "there's more than enough pratie
for everyone. Why don't you all take some?"

So the villagers sawed and chopped and carted off huge pieces of potato while Jamie sat on the stone wall and watched.

All winter long, everyone had potato to eat, and eat and eat until no one wanted to see or hear of potato again.

In the spring Jamie said, "I saved a potato eye for a seed and it's just about time to plant it."

"Oh, no!" the villagers all cried. "If you promise not to plant it, Jamie, we'll promise before St. Patrick and all the saints to see that you and Eileen always have plenty to cook and eat. We don't want another giant pratie around here."

Jamie smiled and agreed. What a perfect life for a lazy man!

"And so you see, darlin' Eileen," Jamie told her, "I wasn't such a fool with that leprechaun after all." And Eileen had to admit that Jamie O'Rourke was right.